WHERE'S THE UNICORN?

AN EPIC ADVENTURE

ILLUSTRATED BY PAUL MORAN

WRITTEN BY JONNY LEIGHTON

COVER DESIGN BY ANGIE ALLISON
DESIGN BY JACK CLUCAS

Michael O'Mara Books Limited

INTRODUCTION

The unicorns of Rainbow Valley are worried. The beautiful flowers and trees are turning grey, the streams have lost their sparkle and the sky is dark and gloomy. The magic of their home is disappearing ...

But Ruby, the leader of the gang, has had an idea. She's heard of an ancient, lost city called Unicopolis, which is home to countless magical treasures that might help restore the beauty of their home. They just have to find it.

Spot the seven unicorns in every scene as they set off on their epic adventure. Work your way through and keep an eye out for the 'epic finds', special items and people that will help the unicorns on their way. You will find all of the answers, plus extra things to spot, at the back of the book.

WHERE'S THE
UNICORN?
AN EPIC ADVENTURE

THE UNICORNS OF RAINBOW VALLEY

LEAF

Leaf is a born adventurer. He's always up for a challenge and never seems to be afraid of anything. He'll be the first one crossing rickety rope bridges or scaling scary heights, showing the unicorns how it's done.

RUBY

Ruby is the leader of the unicorns of Rainbow Valley. She loves to show her friends the way, so she can't wait to take them on an epic adventure across the world to find the lost city of Unicopolis.

SNOWFLAKE

Snowflake is a sensitive soul and the wisest of the unicorns. He's interested in the history of Unicopolis and the strange and magical artefacts they hope to find there. He'll also know just what to do in a tight spot.

BLOSSOM

Blossom is the most sensible of all the unicorns. She'll be the one examining the map closely and making sure the unicorns are going in the right direction. Nothing gets past brainy Blossom.

LUNA

Luna is the fastest of all the unicorns – and she'll need all of that speed for this epic adventure. Whether it's running away from baddies or being the first to find an epic item, no one can do it faster than her.

STARDUST

Stardust is always happy and smiley, nothing gets this unicorn down. He'll be cracking jokes and making the other unicorns giggle the whole way, whether they're in a haunted castle or a gloomy ancient tomb.

AMETHYST

Amethyst is super smart. If there's a secret code to crack or an ancient unicorn language to decipher, she'll be right on the case. She loves adventuring, too, and can't wait to get started!

LIBRARY LORE

The unicorns start their adventure in a magnificent library run by unicorn scholars and their many magical helpers.

Amethyst has caused a bit of a commotion, sending a load of books flying everywhere. Blossom wants to help one of the unicorn experts with her important work. She hopes it will help her find out more about Unicopolis.

Spot the unicorns and the epic find, a book that will tell them more about Unicopolis.

GALLERY GOSSIP

The unicorns need to meet a contact from a secret unicorn society. They've chosen the busy Centre Pompidou in Paris – hopefully no one in the crowd will overhear them.

Leaf admires all of the colourful modern art on display. Stardust is determined to pop one of the unicorn balloons with his horn – if only he can get one before they float away.

Spot the unicorns and the epic find, the unicorn society contact wearing a rainbow scarf.

CREEPY CASTLE

The unicorns have been told that the map to Unicopolis has been split up into three pieces and scattered across the globe. The first piece can be found in a haunted Scottish castle.

Ruby is playing chase with one of the ghosts, but it keeps disappearing through the walls. Snowflake is joining the tour group – they're all in for a very spooky evening.

Spot the unicorns and the epic find, a case that contains the first piece of the map.

UNDER THE SEA

The next piece of the map is located deep below the surface of the Mediterranean Sea. It's hidden among the shipwrecks that litter the ruins of the legendary lost city of Atlantis.

Snowflake loves looking at all of the ancient statues and buildings down there. Ruby is just enjoying swimming with all of the colourful fishes and beautiful mermaids.

Spot the unicorns and the epic item, a case that contains the second piece of the map.

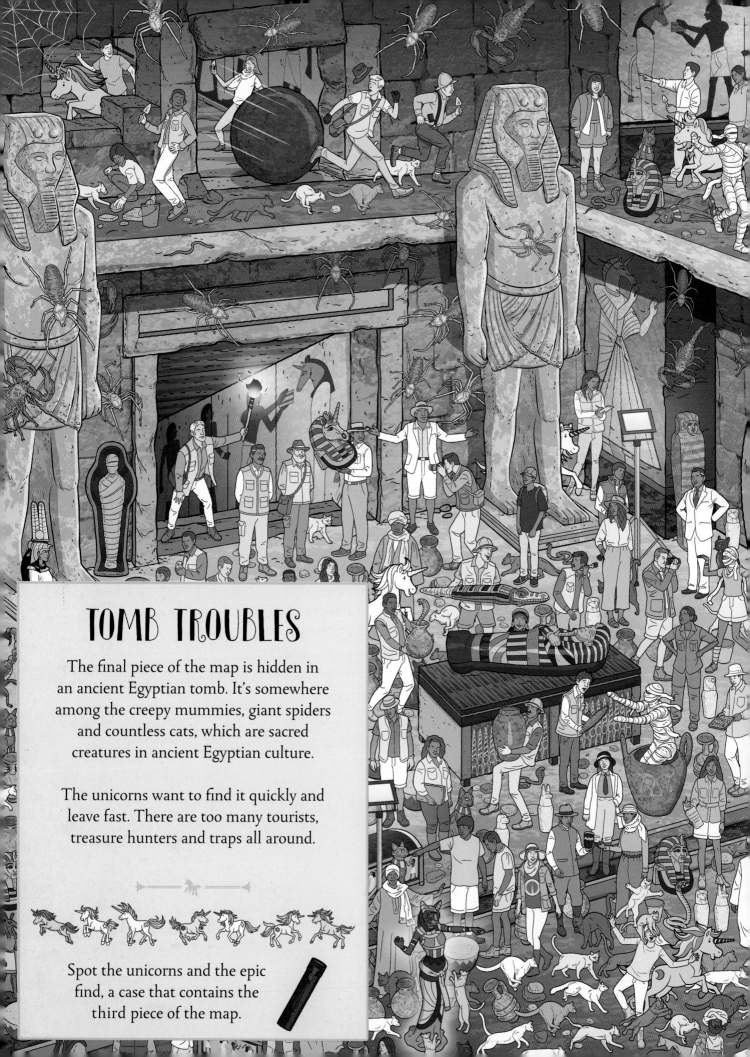

TOMB TROUBLES

The final piece of the map is hidden in an ancient Egyptian tomb. It's somewhere among the creepy mummies, giant spiders and countless cats, which are sacred creatures in ancient Egyptian culture.

The unicorns want to find it quickly and leave fast. There are too many tourists, treasure hunters and traps all around.

Spot the unicorns and the epic find, a case that contains the third piece of the map.

NORDIC FOREST

The unicorns have all the pieces of the map to Unicopolis, but it's written in an old language they can't read. They go to a mystical forest to find a stone which will help them translate it.

Amethyst is having a great time making friends with Sleipnir the eight-legged horse, a '*jötunn*' (giant) and a '*fossegrim*' (music-playing water sprite).

Spot the unicorns and the epic find, a stone carved with a double-headed unicorn.

THE DESERT DOORWAY

The map leads the unicorns to the entrance to Unicopolis – a huge, stone doorway built into a rocky canyon in the desert.

But they're met by Avarice Pym – a notorious treasure hunter – and his minions, the Grey Order. These baddies have been following the unicorns all the way here, and now they'll try to steal the magic treasure for themselves!

Spot the unicorns and the epic find, Grey Order leader, Avarice Pym.

OUT IN THE COLD

The Grey Order don't want the unicorns to find the treasure, so they trick them into taking a very wrong turn. Before they know it, they've ended up in Antarctica.

Ruby must lead them back to safety, but first she has to get past a lot of squawking penguins. Snowflake doesn't mind the birds too much, it's the out-of-this-world visitors he's worried about.

Spot the unicorns and the epic find, a walkie-talkie they can use to call for help.

OCEAN RESCUE

Phew! Someone has come to the unicorns' aid. A member of the secret unicorn society has sent a rescue party to save them.

Blossom has always wanted to swim with dolphins, and now she's got the chance. Leaf is going to try his hand at sailing a yacht. He's such an adventurer, he's sure to get the hang of it in no time.

Spot the unicorns and the epic find, a rainbow-striped life buoy.

JIUFEN VILLAGE

At last, the unicorns make it to dry land. They've been dropped off at Jiufen Village in Taiwan. The busy streets are full of tourists and locals shopping, eating and having fun.

Luna is hungry – all that adventuring has made her stomach rumble. Stardust is heading into the crowd to make some new friends before they have to head off once again.

Spot the unicorns and the epic find, a small statue of a golden unicorn.

TREKKING TIME

To get back to the entrance to Unicopolis, the unicorns must trek across the Gobi Desert. Luckily, they're not the only ones – they join what's known as a desert caravan to help them cross the challenging landscape.

Luna fancies her chances in a race with a Bactrian camel. Snowflake is going to curl up in a cosy blanket and look at the stars.

Spot the unicorns and the epic find, the Grey Order spy who is watching their every move.

IN THE EVERGLADES

The unicorns have been rumbled. The Grey Order have found them once again and chased them as far as the Everglades in Florida, USA.

Ruby wants to make friends with the band playing bluegrass music by the water. The rest of the unicorns are far too busy dodging hungry alligators, slithering snakes and Grey Order baddies to dance.

Spot the unicorns and the epic find, a compass that will guide them back to the Desert Doorway.

LAVA CAVE CHAOS

The unicorns have made it back to the Desert Doorway, the gateway to Unicopolis. Inside it's like another world. There are magma monsters, stone trolls and even a clan of lizard people.

Leaf is in his element – he loves jumping over the fiery river. Snowflake really wants to learn more about the amazing creatures.

Spot the unicorns and the epic find, a precious emerald unicorn horn.

THE LOST CITY

The lost city of Unicopolis is not quite as 'lost' as the unicorns thought it would be. Many mythical creatures have made it their home and it's actually quite crowded.

Amethyst marvels at the phoenixes made of pure fire. Stardust spots lots of winged horses flying through the sky – he wishes he had wings so he could join in, too.

Spot the unicorns and the epic find, a rare bird with a rainbow crest.

CITADEL STEPS

The magical artefact the unicorns need is at the top of a tall tower. First they have to get past the dragons, ogres, dwarves and elves that have taken over the ancient citadel.

Amethyst is getting a good workout, running up all those steps. Ruby is not a fan of some of the giant creepy crawlies scuttling about. The sooner they get to the top, the better.

Spot the unicorns and the epic find, a special rainbow shield.

TREASURE TROVE

Finally, the unicorns have found the treasure
at the top of the tower in Unicopolis's citadel.
They're amazed by the ancient treasures
of this lost unicorn civilization.

Avarice Pym has got there first, but the magic
sceptre in the centre of the room is a decoy.
Only unicorns can wield unicorn magic –
thieves are turned to stone!

Spot the unicorns and the epic find,
the real magical sceptre that will
restore Rainbow Valley's magic.

RAINBOW VALLEY

The unicorns did it! They found the treasure which restored the magic of Rainbow Valley. That means it's time for a big unicorn party.

Unicorns have come from all around to celebrate – Ruby has never seen so many different types and colours. Leaf is thrilled to be making so many new friends. He just hopes that there's enough cake to go round.

Spot the unicorns and the epic find, a unique rainbow-striped balloon.

ANSWERS

LIBRARY LORE

GALLERY GOSSIP

CREEPY CASTLE

SPOTTER'S CHECKLIST

A skeleton wearing a crown ☐

A unicorn ghost ☐

A ghost tossing the caber ☐

A tourist taking a photo ☐

A skeleton with its kilt pulled down ☐

Two smiling ghosts ☐

A skeleton lying in bed ☐

A skeleton playing the bagpipes ☐

A ghost playing the bagpipes ☐

A ghost dropping a broom ☐

SPOTTER'S CHECKLIST

A mermaid stealing a flipper ☐

Two orange octopuses ☐

A diver inside the shipwreck ☐

Three ghostly water unicorns ☐

Two ghostly soldiers riding seahorses ☐

A sea god with a trident ☐

Five sharks ☐

A sea goddess with tentacles ☐

A treasure chest with gold coins inside ☐

Nine scuba divers ☐

UNDER THE SEA

TOMB TROUBLES

SPOTTER'S CHECKLIST

A mummified crocodile ☐

A unicorn mummy ☐

A goddess with a cat's face ☐

A god with a falcon's face ☐

A red and yellow striped sarcophagus ☐

A man with a red eye patch ☐

A snake coming out of a pot ☐

A giant snake ☐

Two dog statues ☐

A man writing on a blue clipboard ☐

NORDIC FOREST

THE DESERT DOORWAY

OUT IN THE COLD

SPOTTER'S CHECKLIST

A green helicopter ☐

An orca whale ☐

A unicorn statue ☐

A dog with a red neckerchief ☐

A penguin inside a boat ☐

Three castaways ☐

Three sharks ☐

A woman with a purple life jacket ☐

A man caught in a boat's rigging ☐

A red helicopter ☐

OCEAN RESCUE

SPOTTER'S CHECKLIST

A unicorn kite ☐

A boy wearing a blue unicorn T-shirt ☐

A pink parasol ☐

A blue bicycle ☐

A waitress spilling a meal ☐

A boy doing a handstand ☐

A man playing the guitar ☐

A broken green vase ☐

Seven floating lanterns ☐

A dog begging for a treat ☐

JIUFEN VILLAGE

TREKKING TIME

SPOTTER'S CHECKLIST

A man juggling with fire ☐

Someone dressed as a unicorn ☐

Two men playing instruments ☐

A red tea chest ☐

A man carrying a carpet ☐

A red-and-blue-striped blanket ☐

A man falling off a camel ☐

A man dropping a tea set ☐

A campfire ☐

A big white camel with reins ☐

IN THE EVERGLADES

SPOTTER'S CHECKLIST

A woman feeding a crocodile ☐

A man with red-and-white stripy socks ☐

Two people playing banjos ☐

A giant snake ☐

A Grey Order flag ☐

A man caught on a fishing rod ☐

A woman in yellow dungarees ☐

Two hovercraft ☐

A man in a red-and-yellow shirt ☐

A man wearing red gloves ☐

SPOTTER'S CHECKLIST

A rickety bridge ☐

A pink lizard person ☐

A fire extinguisher ☐

A lizard with spiky blue hair ☐

A bright-blue giant frog ☐

A lizard sitting on a ladder ☐

A stone troll eating lava ☐

A blue horn-shaped gemstone ☐

A double-headed unicorn symbol ☐

A yellow horn-shaped gemstone ☐

LAVA CAVE CHAOS

THE LOST CITY

SPOTTER'S CHECKLIST

A part-lion, part-snake, part-goat ☐

Four giant snails ☐

Two huge unicorn statues ☐

Six blue goblins ☐

A woman on a flying deer ☐

Five cockerels with black wings ☐

Two fauns playing flutes ☐

Two eagle women ☐

A family of Cyclopses ☐

A double-headed unicorn symbol ☐

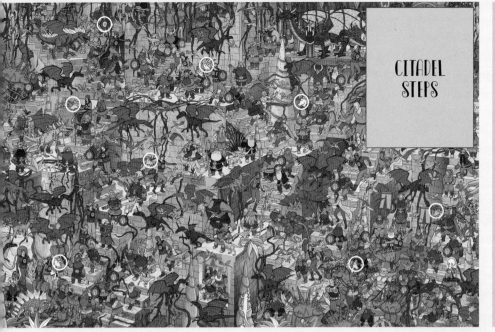

CITADEL STEPS

SPOTTER'S CHECKLIST

A giant pink flower ☐

A blue dragon ☐

Two purple-and-yellow banners ☐

An alien ☐

A giant red-and-yellow dragon ☐

A Grey Order baddy caught in a web ☐

A dwarf covered in dragon snot ☐

A purple, horned, one-eyed Cyclops ☐

A white, horned lizard ☐

A dwarf with a pink beard ☐

SPOTTER'S CHECKLIST

A statue of a one-eyed man ☐

A unicorn helmet ☐

A throne ☐

A pink carved centaur ☐

A purple unicorn with a green mane ☐

A silver-blue unicorn with a red mane ☐

A red unicorn-horn banner ☐

A red unicorn-horn shield ☐

A gigantic green gemstone ☐

A gigantic pink gemstone ☐

TREASURE TROVE

RAINBOW VALLEY

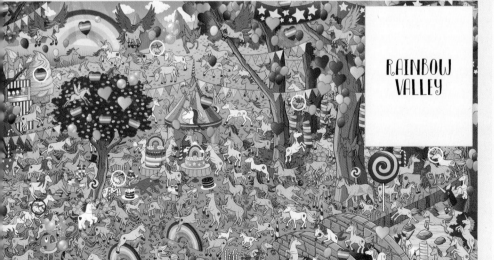

SPOTTER'S CHECKLIST

A unicorn in a white onesie ☐

A unicorn scuba diving ☐

A unicorn in a magician's outfit ☐

An orange unicorn with yellow bows ☐

A bubble machine ☐

A unicorn falling off a space hopper ☐

A unicorn dressed as a superhero ☐

An ice-cream stall ☐

Cupcakes on a tiered cake stand ☐

A cake with rainbow-striped layers ☐

Published in Great Britain in 2021 by Michael O'Mara Books Limited,
9 Lion Yard, Tremadoc Road, London SW4 7NQ

W www.mombooks.com   f Michael O'Mara Books   🐦 @OMaraBooks   📷 @omarabooks

A CIP catalogue record for this book is available from the British Library.

ISBN: 978-1-78929-308-1

1 3 5 7 9 10 8 6 4 2

This book was printed in July 2021 by Shenzhen Wing King Tong
Paper Products Co. Ltd., Shenzhen, Guangdong, China.

Papers used by Michael O'Mara Books are natural, recyclable products made
from wood grown in sustainable forests. The manufacturing processes
conform to the environmental regulations of the country of origin.